LOOK AND FIND®

Worlds of Wonder

Illustrated by Art Mawhinney

© Disney Enterprises, Inc.

This publication may not be reproduced in whole
or in part by any means whatsoever without
written permission from the copyright owners.
Permission is never granted for commercial purposes.

Published by Louis Weber, C.E.O.
Publications International, Ltd.
7373 North Cicero Avenue
Lincolnwood, Illinois 60712

Ground Floor, 59 Gloucester Place
London W1U 8JJ

Customer Service: 1-800-595-8484
or customer_service@pilbooks.com

www.pilbooks.com

Manufactured in China.

p i kids is a registered trademark of
Publications International, Ltd.
Look and Find is a registered trademark of
Publications International, Ltd., in the United States and in Canada.

8 7 6 5 4 3 2 1

ISBN-13: 978-1-4127-6490-2
ISBN-10: 1-4127 6490-4

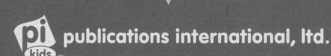

publications international, ltd.

King Triton held a royal concert to present his youngest daughter Ariel and her beautiful singing voice. But Ariel and Flounder forgot—and now they're late! Will they make it back in time?

Search the stage to find Ariel's six singing sisters.

At midnight, Cinderella will lose a glass slipper. But some other maidens at the ball have already lost their accessories! Can you help these ladies find what they have misplaced?

Her earring

Her cape

Her fan

Her glove

Her necklace

Her purse

To help Belle feel at home in his castle, the Beast shows her the library. Since Belle loves books, she will have a wonderful time reading these.

The Beginner's Guide to Chords and Quarter Notes

The Firebreathers

How Does Your Garden Grow

Gadgets, Gizmos, and Good Ideas

A History of Hocus Pocus

It's no wonder the Fairy Godmothers had to use their magic to make Briar Rose's birthday cake. Just look at the mess they made trying to bake without their wands! Hopefully these treats taste better than they look.

Don't-scream ice-cream sundae

Bleu cheesecake

Apple turnover

Sunken soufflé

Pity-fours

Ariel loves exploring sunken ships and gathering treasures from the human world. It seems the fish love to, too! You'll need to take a deep breath to keep up with these fancy fish. But you better hurry…the shark is coming!

Crowned cod

Sapphire bluegill

Ruby-red snapper

Goldfish

Silver swordfish

When it comes to the Seven Dwarfs, one is never enough of anything! Find the following things the Seven Dwarfs have brought to celebrate Snow White's health and happiness.

 Seven gifts

Seven cakes

 Seven invitations

Seven bouquets

 Seven framed photos

Despite the cold weather, even the birds can't help but notice that Belle is warming up to the Beast. Besides your scarf and mittens, you'll need bird-watching binoculars to find these feathered friends.

Red-head robin

Hummingbird duet

Love birds

Bald eagle

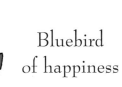

Bluebird of happiness

Cinderella is thrilled with the dress her little friends have made for her! In addition to the pretty pink frock, the mice and birds also came up with these creations.

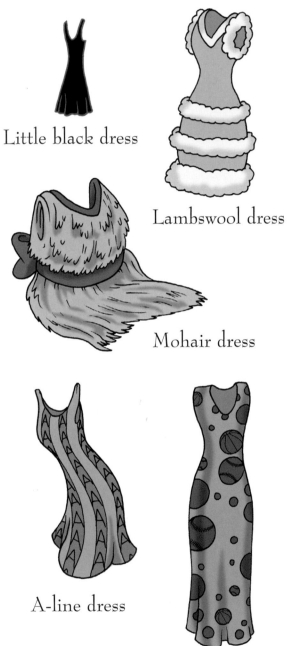

Little black dress

Lambswool dress

Mohair dress

A-line dress

Ball gown

At the undersea concert, find these musically inclined sea creatures.

Hammerhead Dulcimer

Clambourine

Lutefish

Pianoctopus

Guitarpon

Hurry! It's almost midnight! Go back to the ballroom and find nine timepieces.

Search the stacks for other items that will make Belle feel at home.

♥ Picture of home
♥ Horse figurine
♥ Pen and paper set
♥ Flowers
♥ Portrait of her dad

It's Briar Rose's Sweet Sixteen! Sift through the floury scene to find 16 of the following things.

♥ Flowers
♥ Candles
♥ Hearts
♥ Bows
♥ Birds

It takes a long time for an oyster to make a pearl. Swim back through the sunken ship to spot these pearly pieces that have come back to the sea.

- ♥ Pearl earrings
- ♥ Pearl ring
- ♥ Pearl bracelet
- ♥ Pearl brooch
- ♥ String of pearls

Snow White will miss the Seven Dwarfs so much, she's given each of them a gift to remember her by.

A handkerchief for Sneezy

A glasses case for Doc

A mirror for Grumpy

A gold star for Dopey

A blanket for Bashful

A teddy bear for Happy

A pillow for Sleepy

No two snowflakes are exactly alike ... or are they? Find seven matching pairs of snowflakes.

Cinderella's friends have an eye for fashion, but when it comes to a ball, not everything goes! Go back and search the attic for these things one should NOT wear to such a fancy occasion.

- ♥ Chef's hat
- ♥ Artist's beret
- ♥ Bloomers
- ♥ Hoop skirt
- ♥ Riding boots